DIARY OF NATE THE MINECRAFT NINJA 2

Write Blocked

Write Blocked Publishing

Dedicated To The Fans That Leave Reviews

Keep It Up!

CONTENTS

Stay Up To Date With Write Blocked:

Follow Me on Twitter: https://twitter.com/writeblocked

Follow Me on Instagram: https://www.instagram.com/writeblocked/

(NEW) Join the group on Goodreads: https://www.goodreads.com/group/1173039

Join the Fan Club on discord: https://discord.gg/FAFWz7g

Subscribe to my Newsletter: https://tinyletter.com/WriteBlocked

Diary of Nate the Minecraft Ninja 2

A Doctorate in Evil

Write Blocked

> *"It is difficult to catch a black cat in a dark room, especially when it's not there."*

\- **Confucius**

CHAPTER 1: LOST AND FOUND

I've been pretty happy ever since I completed my first official Ender Ninja mission. I stopped the delivery of a mysterious package to someone called Dr. Herobrine. Not only that, but I also defeated the evil pillager brothers, Tick and Tock.

The police found them unconscious in the warehouse where I defeated them in, and now they're in jail.

Not bad for a kid ninja on his first mission.

But now, as I wait for my next mission, I'm back to being regular old Nate Noonan. Just an ordinary kid in ordinary middle school.

At least I have my best friend, Katie Kennedy, to help me get through the day. I thought we were ready for class, but Katie was still searching through her locker.

"How's it going over there?" I asked.

My locker sat next to Katie's locker. Katie shoveled through loose paper, mismatched pens, and blocks of red sand from our field trip to the Badlands Biome. She looked really distracted, and it didn't even look like she heard my question.

"Katie...?" I asked again. "I can help if you want."

I closed my locker.

Pens — *check.*

Class books — *check.*

Homework — *check.*

Apple — *check.*

I was ready for school.

"Oh, I'm good," Katie finally spoke up.

I couldn't see Katie's face because she had buried her head so deep in her locker. Whatever she was looking for, it must be important.

"I probably have an extra whatever-it-is you're looking for...." I said while I peered into her locker.

I was so curious, *too* curious. Katie pulled her head back and slammed the locker door shut.

Meanwhile, I narrowly avoided a broken nose or worse.

"Noodle," Katie said.

Neither of us said it aloud, but Katie and I mentally screamed. Our perfect Monday morning was struck with disaster…a lost chicken.

"Noodle is gone again!" Katie said. "I usually don't mind when he goes out to explore, but I wish he would wait till classes start and the halls clear."

"There are too many people around now," I said as I looked at the hallway filled with other students, teachers, and janitors.

"Exactly!" Katie frowned.

"Katie," I said and clapped my hand together. "I vow to call upon my ninja training to search for your Noodle and will not be defeated in my journey for the lost little chicken."

Then I bowed as a show of honor in ninja culture.

"Sure ya will," Katie replied, holding back a giggle.

"Are you laughing?"

"No."

"Katie, I WILL find that chicken."

"I have no doubt."

"Really?"

"Yeah, because if you don't, you'll forever be known as Samurai Wack, the only living legend to be defeated by a baby chicken."

"First of all, ninjas and samurais are two different things. Second of all, did you hear that?" I placed my finger behind my ear as if I had heard a clue in the faint distance.

Katie looked around, trying to see the noise. We scanned the rows of lockers, studying the numbers. We looked through the small crowds of students gathered together like bundles of cows around a freshwater spring.

"What?" Katie asked.

I waited to tell her.

"What, Nate?" She asked again. Katie's impatience grew and slowly surfaced to her face.

"You called me a legend," I said.

"What? I—That's not the point."

"Not to you, it isn't."

"Nate, we have class in like fifteen minutes. That's fifteen minutes of halls filled with students and one tiny chicken trying to hide from them all."

"Don't worry, the *legend* is on the case," I puffed my chest out and smiled.

"Okay, but you're not a legend."

"Not until I find the chicken?" I asked.

"Find Noodle first, and we'll see...." Katie replied.

I didn't think this was how my week would start—chicken hunting before first period. As a ninja though, I always have to be ready for the unexpected. Maybe I could lure Noodle out of his hiding spot.

I scanned the hall for any sign of a chicken... feathers, high-pitched clucking, or even tiny, cubed poops. More classmates walked in through the entrance at the west end of the hallway.

As we get closer and closer to classes starting, more and more kids will be rushing in through the doors, which meant more chances of Noodle getting caught and possibly getting kicked out of the school. Not to mention the trouble Katie is going to be in.

My eyes passed over the surroundings, and there were no signs of feathers. I wasn't able to hear any clucking or see any mini poops.

My eyes landed on Locker 111. Number 111. Of course, the only locker in the school I know the number of, other than mine and Katies.

Locker 111 is Min Mei's locker. I have known Min since elementary school. Since first grade. She wore glasses then—thin, blue, and silver frames with square glass.

Min stood in front of her locker with her girls. It's easy to see why Min Mei has so many friends. She's an easy-going, kind, beautiful, talented artist, and musician. There's nothing that Min Mei has ever been bad at. So of course, she's also incredibly popular.

While Min hung out with her friends around their lockers, I kept eye-hunting for a chicken. But I also kept glancing back at Min.

I wonder if she still knows my name.

I know she knew my name at some point. It was like a year ago. During our physical education class, Min was picked as team leader for one of the teams. After picking all her friends, she had finally said it, maybe for the first time—she said, *Nate... Nate... Na* —

"—te... Nate. Nate!" Katie said.

She pulled on my backpack, and I was back in reality.

"I found Noodle...." Katie said.

"Huh? What? Where?"

She pointed down the north end of the hall, right at a screaming and panicking Robbie Ragsdill. Robbie is the star footblock player for our school and the meanest kid on the block. He loves to pick on me.

"There's a chicken in my locker!" He yelled.

The kids in his hall laughed at him.

"I'm not kidding!" Robbie yelled. "There's a tiny chicken in my locker, and it bit me!"

According to what Katie told me, Noodle busted into Robbie's locker, clucking and squealing. Robbie, who was flustered, tried to grab at Noodle. Unfortunately for Robbie, Noodle only likes Katie for some reason, so when Robbie reached into his locker, Noodle pecked his finger.

Thankfully, so far, no one else saw Noodle other than Robbie.

Katie and I quickly ran over to Robbie's locker. Robbie was blindly punching all the old gym clothes in his locker, hoping to catch the chicken.

"Robbie, behind you, it's the little chicken's big mama!" I shouted.

Robbie quickly turned in a panic, and Katie

reached into his locker and grabbed Noodle. The art of distraction is, like, lesson number one of Ender Ninja training.

"Hey! There's no chicken here," Robbie said as he turned back to face me.

"Just like there's no chicken in your locker," I laughed.

"You scrawny little nerd, there *is* a chicken in my locker," Robbie reached back into his locker and started emptying it.

His gym clothes and old thought-to-be-lost homework assignments littered the ground around him.

Robbie's gym underwear was the last to leave his now empty locker.

"Wow," Katie said, "I didn't even know they made those for guys...."

"...I didn't even know guys could wear that," I replied.

"But...but I did...I saw it...I swear...it was right here," Robbie stuck his head inside his empty locker.

"Hey Robbie, maybe you're seeing a ghost chicken," Katie yelled down the hall as we made our way back to our lockers. "Maybe if you didn't eat so many chicken nuggets, this wouldn't happen to you!"

Robbie was too confused to think of a retort and just scratched his head.

It was true. Robbie has always had a thing for the nuggets.

Katie and I reached our lockers, and Katie placed Noodle back inside.

"If you get caught, we'll be in big trouble," Katie warned Noodle. "You have to stay low."

"But if you want to bother someone, you couldn't have picked a better person than Robbie," I added.

"Don't encourage him!" Katie complained as she closed the locker shut.

With Noodle secured, we started to head to our first class of the day.

"Well, Ninja Nate…" Katie said, "I'm counting this one as *my* find."

"What? How?"

"You were lookin' at Min; off in Minland, state of Minsillvania, south of the capital Min city, on a little street the neighborhood calls Min Lane, zip code xoxoxo."

"Point made," I replied, with my cheeks turning red. "But if anything, Robbie found the chicken."

We both started to laugh.

"*If anything,*" Katie said, "technically, Noodle found Robbie."

We continued laughing at Robbie's embarrassing expense.

"But on a technicality," Katie said. "We'll call it a draw."

"You drive a hard bargain for not being a ninja," I replied.

"Remember to keep it zipped if Principal Patrick starts to get nosey. As far as he's concerned, the school is haunted by a ghost chicken," Katie said, tugging at my backpack again. "C'mon, let's go. We're goin' to be late!"

I looked back down to the end of the hallway, but between Robbie and Noodle, and all the craziness that those two brought down our hallway, I couldn't see Min anymore. It was either too crowded or she was already gone.

"Silence is golden."

- **Nintoku**

CHAPTER 2: MIN-SION IMPOSSIBLE

When first-period break began, Katie and I headed back to our lockers. Katie looked inside to find Noodle innocently munching on some melon seeds. Katie gave Noodle a suspicious look.

Katie's locker slammed closed again. I don't think her locker has ever NOT slammed shut. Katie had an extremely slammable locker, or Katie herself couldn't help but be a natural slammer herself.

She would make a terrible ninja with how loud she is. Has Katie been stealthy? Hardly. Did she dress in all black? Far from it. Has Katie ever snuck out of the house at night? Well, yes, actually, and on the regular, but that doesn't automatically make her a ninja. And yet she has made herself my sidekick.

I remember when I talked to Sensei Setsuo about my first mission, and I had to tell him about Katie finding out my identity. He was initially upset, but after I introduced them, he realized how impossible it would've been to hide my identity from a friend like Katie. He also had an explanation for Katie's *helping hand*. He said:

Nate, your proficiency and aptitude grow like underwater kelp on supple soil. And just as the dirt blocks on which the kelp grows, you must plant your feet into the soil of the community with an open heart. Like a flower, to blossom, you must accept that you are connected in life and roots with those that grow around you.

Sensei Setsuo is a wise man, but honestly, all I could think of when he talked to me was how much I love eating dried kelp.

It's the perfect snack.

I saw Min Mei again. She was standing by her locker, exchanging her books for the next class. I wondered if Min would make an excellent ninja. We could make the perfect pair. She's gentle, she's confident, she's smart, she's—

"So are ya gonna go over there or just creep on her between first and second period?" Katie asked. "Maybe you should ask her to the Fall Ball."

Of course, Katie knows exactly what's on my mind today. She always does.

"Do you think that'll work?" I asked her.

Katie chuckled.

"Yeah, of course. Last year I would've never imagined you would end up stuffing Robbie in a locker, and now look at you—you can do anything." Katie said.

"First of all, he stuffed himself into that locker. And second of all...I can't," I said.

"Nate, you're a ninja-in-training. I've watched you do front flips without a trampoline and absorb the fist of a thirty-year-old pillager with your face. I think you can ask Min to the Fall Ball," Katie said.

"Haha, yeah, I'll just go spouting my ninja training all through school, so everyone knows and my vow of secrecy to the Ender Ninjas is broken. No, thank you."

"If only you could tell people you're a ninja now...." Katie replied.

"But I can't, so there's no way I can just go *ninja* my way into a date for the Fall Ball."

"I mean, you can still impress her without revealing you're a ninja. Look, Nate, if you want to, go now. It's the best opportunity to impress her friends and ask Min out to the Fall Ball. Just go in, ask her, and get out before you get weird," Katie told me.

I took a deep breath and started walking

toward Min with Katie's words in the back of my mind.

When do I ever get weird? I thought. *I never get weird.*

Using my cool new ninja skills, I slinked down the hall toward Min with my back against the lockers. If I say so myself, I was practically invisible to the chaos around me. I was so invisible that—

WHAM!

Some sixth-grader slammed his locker open right in front of me. Fortunately, I stopped the locker door with my face.

"Oh, hey!" the sixth-grader said. "I didn't see you there. Sorry."

"Don't worry about it," I groaned, rubbing my face.

After the sixth-grader left, I continued my skulking along the wall. Luckily for me, Min was still at her locker. I would have to hurry because the bell for the next class was about to—

WHAM!

This time the locker that hit me belonged to someone I knew. Claire something. I didn't know much about her other than that she was a friend of Robbie's.

"What?" she said, closing her door to find my face looking back at her. "Oh. Hey…uhh…*you*."

She didn't know my name. That was fine by me. Any friend of Robbie Ragsdill was not a friend of mine.

"It's okay," I said, wondering if my nose was turning red.

Without an apology or another word, she shrugged, spun on her heels, and walked away. I didn't expect anything less from a friend of Robbie's.

What's with my reflexes today? I wondered. *Why is it that just the thought of talking to Min throws my entire brain off balance?*

Thankfully, the gods of hallway traffic unblocked the rest of my path to Min Mei. I used my incredible ninja stealth skills to sneak up on the brood of girls surrounding Min at her locker, practically clucking gossip like chickens.

I was not expecting Min to notice me standing there. But instead, it was like she was waiting for me.

"Hi, Nate," she said, clutching her textbooks close to her chest.

"Oh, hi," I stammered, not knowing what to say next. *Why didn't I practice what to say beforehand?!?* "I just wanted to ask you—" *to the Fall*

Ball, just say it– "how do you like the weather. I mean, what you're doing about the weather. I mean, the weather, how do you like it?"

She began to smile but then just looked confused. "Uh... Fine, I guess."

"Clouds," I said, "do you like clouds? They're so big and blocky, and they're always above us. How weird is that?" *What am I saying?* I was blowing it. I was blowing it so badly—time to ask about the Fall Ball again. "Balls," I blurted out. "I mean, do you like– Er, do you play any sports with balls?" *What is wrong with you, Nate Noonan?*

"You know I'm a cheerleader, Nate," Min said nervously. Her friends had abandoned her to get to class before the bell rang. "I see you at every footblock game."

It was true. I wasn't interested in the game. Robbie Ragsdill owned the field as our star player, but that's not who I went to see.

The bell rang. Both of us were officially late. Min ran off, most likely because she couldn't stand being around me any longer.

I was late, too.

Why don't I go to my locker, stick my head inside and slam the door on it a couple of times? Maybe Katie can help...

"Clouds," I groaned.

"We learn little from victory, much from defeat."

- **Hakuseki**

CHAPTER 3: A SECOND CHANCE

"Clouds?"

"Yeah."

"Wow." Katie and I sat at our usual table on the school lawn outside, having lunch. She tore off pieces of her potato sandwich and tossed it to Noodle, who was hiding under our table. Noodle gobbled up anything he could get his beak on.

Katie usually had something to say about everything. This time, however, I had left her speechless. She started to say something but shut her mouth. Then she started to say something again, stopped, shrugged, and took another bite.

She shook her head. "The weather...*really?*"

"I know, right?"

The sky was overcast and gloomy. A chill in the

air meant we wouldn't be eating outside for much longer before the winter months came sweeping in. It matched my mood exactly.

"So, what do I do now?"

Katie took another bite. "I have no idea. I've never walked up to a girl and said *balls*."

"Don't remind me."

"I don't think I'll have to remind you anytime soon, Nate Noonan," Katie said. "I have a feeling that you'll remember this day for a long, long time."

Maybe I could take Katie to the dance. That would probably be fun. We'll probably just stand in the corner and point and laugh at people.

"Has anyone asked you yet?" I asked Katie.

"You mean, have *I* asked anyone yet?" Katie said, arching an eyebrow. "Girls are allowed to ask people out to the dance too, you know. And to answer your question, no, I haven't."

"Why not?"

She shrugged. "Haven't found the right person, I guess."

She didn't seem too broken up about it. Katie was like that. She lived life her own way, she didn't care about anyone else.

"You going to eat that sea pickle?"

I shook my head, so Katie picked up the pickle my mom had packed for me and tossed it under the table to Noodle, who practically wolfed it down whole. I'm 90% sure I heard that little chicken burp.

"You know what you should do?" Katie asked, pointing a finger at me.

"Go bang my head in the locker again."

Katie aimed her finger in a different direction. "Try again."

I turned to look where Katie was pointing. Min was coming out of the cafeteria, carrying a tray of food. Middle school cafeteria steak never looked so good. Neither did Min. She got prettier every time I looked at her, which was a lot.

Katie used her pointing finger to poke me in the arm several times. "Go get her, champ."

"No," I said. "No way."

"Why not?" Katie shooed Noodle, who was trying to climb up her leg, back under the table."

"What if I say something dumb again?"

"Don't worry about that," Katie said, slightly lifting my spirits. "You'll almost certainly say something stupid," she said, crushing my confidence again. "That's not the point. You're a ninja, right?"

"Yeah."

"You're not afraid of anything, right?"

"Yeah."

"You beat Tick and Tock without breaking a sweat, right?"

"Yeah." That last one wasn't entirely true. I did sweat a little. Okay, maybe more than a little.

"You miss all the shots you never take," She said. "Do or do not. There is no try. And all other metaphors they probably teach you in Ninja school." She waved me away. "Now go. Shoo."

Grudgingly, I stood. I approached Min's table by way of the trash-composter on the other side of the courtyard. There was no reason to get it over with when I could torture myself for as long as possible.

I emptied the remaining half-eaten food from my lunchbox into the trashcan, trying to find another way to stall the inevitable embarrassment of talking to Min again.

She'd probably just say no and laugh in my face anyway.

A parrot landed on the trashcan in front of me. Parrots were how the Ender Ninjas communicated with each other. I didn't understand why they would use such a flamboyant bird to send messages when they could just meet up with each other.

I looked back at Katie and gestured to the bird.

I can't ask Min out now, my expression said. *Sensei needs me.*

Katie rolled her eyes. *Fine, whatever. Let's go.*

"Life is really simple, but man always insists on making it complicated."

\-   **Confucius**

CHAPTER 4: DR. WHO?

In a school the size of ours, it was challenging to find a place to have a truly private conversation, especially with a parrot. But the parrot swooped away from the trashcan and led us to a secluded spot behind the theater building.

Nobody ever went in the theater building except for the drama kids because the drama teacher was bat-bonkers crazy. I've been told that all drama teachers are like that, but that's another story for another time.

Talking to a parrot was always interesting. It spoke in Sensei Setsuo's voice, but it was like trying to have a conversation with a recording, like a music disc in a jukebox. But weirdly enough, Sensei would sometimes predict questions we'd probably ask and when we'll ask them. Spooky.

"Greetings, Nate," the parrot said. "Hello, Katie."

"How did it know I was here?" Katie whispered

to me.

"Because you're always here," the parrot spoke in the slightly annoyed voice Sensei used whenever talking to–or about–Katie.

As I said, it was spooky.

"I've been looking into our friend, Dr. Herobrine," the parrot said.

Dr. Herobrine, if he was even really a doctor, was supposed to receive a large chest of iron ingots and a pumpkin. I intercepted the chest. We didn't know what the parts were for, but they *could* have been for building an Iron Golem. We weren't sure.

"Dr. Herobrine was recently fired as Chief Research Officer at Redstone Industries," the parrot continued.

What's Redstone Industries? I thought.

"Redstone Industries is a technology firm pursuing the goal of world peace through redstone inventions," the parrot said, almost like it read my mind.

Yeah, definitely spooky.

The parrot went on. "Even though we stopped him from receiving the materials before, I believe he has acquired them another way and continues his mission to construct an Iron Golem."

So, Sensei believes that Dr. Herobrine was back to building his Golem. That was something worth looking into.

"I want you to look into this, Nate," the parrot said. "Find out if he is building anything. If he is, figure out what it is. Do you accept this mission? Please respond "yes" or "no," and this messenger will report your answer back to me."

"Yes!" The word practically burst out of Katie's mouth. The parrot didn't respond to Katie, but it looked expectantly at me.

"I will accept this challenge, Sensei," I said. "And I will be successful."

"I knew you would," the parrot said. You could hear the pride in Sensei's voice even when a bird reported it. The parrot shook out its feathers. "Godspeed, Nate. This messenger will ask for seeds in five seconds."

"What does that mean?" Katie asked.

"Seeds? Seeds?" the parrot responded with a more typical parrot voice. "Seeds?"

"What?" I checked my pockets even though I knew I didn't have seeds.

"Seeds? Seeds?" The parrot continued, each time its request became more threatening sounding.

"Seeds?"

Katie quickly reached into her pockets and gave the parrot the remainder of her melon seeds, and the bird took flight, disappearing behind the theater building.

Noodle, who had been silently watching the conversation from the safety of Katie's backpack, squawked angrily.

I noticed a piece of paper left behind where the parrot was standing. I took a look at it, and it looked like an address to Dr. Herobrine's lab.

"So," Katie said in a chipper tone, "when do we leave? I don't have any homework, so I say we head over there after school."

"No," I said flatly.

"What do you mean, *no*?"

"I mean," I said, "that you are not going with me."

"Why not?"

"Because..." I struggled to come up with a reason. "Because you are not a ninja, I don't want you to get hurt."

"Why, Nate Noonan," Katie said, suddenly coy, "I do believe you're sweet on little ol' me."

"What? No! I'm not sweet on you. I'm not sweet on anybody!" It wasn't that Katie wasn't pretty or fun to be around. She was all those things and more. It was just that my heart belonged to another. "...Except Min, maybe."

"Prove it." Katie batted her eyes.

"Fine, you can come along, *again*," I said, and immediately regretted it.

"You won't regret this, Nate Noonan," Katie chirped. I knew I'd just been had. I didn't know how, but I would figure it out.

In the meantime, there was still one more challenge I would have to overcome before I could start my mission.

"Three things cannot be hidden: the sun, the moon, and the truth."

- **Confucius**

CHAPTER 5: REVEALED

After the last bell of the school day rung, it was officially the end of the school day. Which means all the kids in school launched out of the building at rocket speeds, nearly unable to wait until they got home and could play around.

I don't have time for games or anything like that. I had a mission to accomplish. What mission, you ask.

Tracking down Dr. Herobrine to see what he was up to?

Nope. That could wait until later.

I had a much more critical mission first:

Asking Min Mei to the Fall Ball without embarrassing myself.

"Look, there she is," Katie said, pointing at Min, who was giggling with her friends on the way out of school.

Min had the prettiest laugh. She had the prettiest everything, for that matter. Her laugh was beautiful like village bells in the morning.

"Hey, Nate! Overworld to Noonan! Come in, Noonan!" Katie shook me by the arm, waking me from my daydream. "She is going to get away." Sure enough, Min had turned away from her friends and was walking away. "Go get her."

I took a deep breath, gathered my courage, and chased her down. I asked her the big question, and she said, "Of course, I'll go to the Fall Ball with you." And we had a wonderful time.

...That is what I wanted to happen. What actually happened wasn't nearly as fun.

"Hey, loser!" Robbie pushed his way into my path, blocking me from Min. "What do you think you're doing?"

"Leave me alone, Robbie," I said, trying to brush past him.

"Never." He held out a hand and stopped my forward momentum completely.

I could have taken him down. I could have vaulted over his head. I could have tossed him up onto the other side of the road. I probably could have broken some bones too.

Trust me, I *did* want to do all of those things, but I couldn't divulge my secret to anyone. Showing off my ninja abilities now would be a big violation of the Ninja Code. No one could know my secret.

"I figured out your little secret," Robbie said. "I figured out exactly who you are and what your big mission is!"

That stopped me cold. Min would have to wait. "What are you talking about, Robbie?"

He stared down at me with an evil smile. "I've seen you sneaking around school, trying to hide and stuff, not let anyone see you. But I saw you. I'm not dumb, you know."

That remained to be seen, but it looked like he had figured out that I was a ninja. Maybe I could bluff my way out. Afterall, ninjas are masters of deception.

"I don't know what you're talking about, Robbie."

"Yeah, right. Sneaking around won't help you out now. I know your secret is that you're trying to ask Min Mei out for the dance, runt. Don't pretend you're not."

I took a deep sigh of relief. On the one hand, it was nice to know that my secret life as a ninja was still safe. On the other hand, this conversation wasn't getting me any closer to Min.

"Ba-GAWK!" I knew that sound.

Noodle was on the loose again.

Robbie's eyes darted around us. "Did you hear that?"

His face was a mask of panic. He looked genuinely afraid. I could use that to my advantage.

"Hear what?" I asked.

"The chicken!"

"What chicken? I don't hear a chicken," I lied.

"Ba-GAWK!" Noodle came flapping around the corner of the building with Katie behind him at a dead sprint.

Noodle was fast. I guess that's why he shows up in the oddest places.

In the split second that it took Robbie to turn around and look for where the noise was coming from, I motioned Katie to slow down and act casual. By the time Robbie spotted Noodle, Katie was strolling along, whistling without a care in the world and looking up at the clouds.

Noodle, in the meantime, charged Robbie. Noodle didn't like Robbie any more than I did. Noodle leaped at his feet, pecking at him.

"Gah! Get the chicken off me! Get it off me!"

Robbie swatted at Noodle, never quite being able to make contact. You'd think that, as a quarterback, he'd have better reflexes.

"What chicken?" I asked, ignoring the fluttering. "I don't see a chicken. Katie, do you see a chicken?"

"Nope, no chickens here," she said, acting confused. "Who sees a chicken?"

Robbie ducked Noodle's attack, swatting at the chicken again. "You don't see this?"

"See what?" Katie said.

"Are you okay, Robbie?" I asked. "You look like you've seen a ghost."

The color immediately drained out of Robbie's face as it turned from panic mode to pure terror. He took off running toward the school.

"Ghost chicken!" he screamed. He rushed back inside, with Noodle right behind him.

Katie and I stood there a moment to watch them go. Then we both burst into laughter so hard that my sides hurt. When I recovered enough to wipe the tears away, I saw that there was nobody around.

Fortunately, that meant that probably nobody

had seen the entire exchange. Unfortunately, that also included Min.

I had missed Min again.

"When a ninja moves, a sound is not made."
-    **Miyamoto Musashi**

CHAPTER 6: BREAKING AND ENTERING

An hour later, and after quite a bit of walking and jogging, Katie and I were standing next to a nondescript three-story building in a business park a few miles away from school.

I had stuffed my ninja outfit, the head-to-toe black garb worn by all the Ender Ninjas, into my backpack beforehand and was slipping into it when Katie rolled up wearing her backpack. Only hers had Noodle poking his head out of it. He wasn't the only thing in Katie's backpack, but I'll get to that later.

"Are you ready?" Katie asked excitedly.

"Meh," I said, shrugging my shoulders. "Just another day in the life of a ninja. Breaking and entering into a supervillain's super lair is just another Monday for me."

I always tried to keep my cool when I was dressed as a ninja, but being a ninja on a mission was super-cool. I highly recommend trying it if a master sensei recruits you to be their apprentice.

I was giddy with excitement, although I tried not to show it.

Katie wasn't buying it. "Uh-huh, sure," she said with one eyebrow raised. "What's the plan?"

Katie always wondered what the plan was and what was her part in it. It was my job to keep her safe while letting her feel valued. "You guard the front door. If anyone comes out, throw Noodle at them and hide."

She gave me a thumbs up and then a snappy salute. "You got it, chief!"

She quietly walked around the corner of the building and disappeared.

That was easier than usual, I thought.

Usually, Katie would nag me about joining the mission until I gave in. Then would make things more complicated than they needed to be. I figured that giving her a job to begin with would keep her safe and, more importantly, out of my hair.

Focusing my attention back on the job at hand, I wondered how I would climb up the building until I could find a way in.

It would be easy to climb the windows but

more dangerous for me as someone could easily spot me if they happened to be close to the window. The element of surprise must always be on a ninja's side. Getting spotted was not the ninja way.

The ninja way would be something way cooler. There was a narrow walkway between the building I was staking out and the one behind it. Being a ninja, I ran silently to the wall of one building and leapt to the one behind it, then leapt back to the first one.

That was the ninja way.

One of the hardest lessons to master while I was undergoing ninja training over the summer was wall jumping, but it is also one of the most useful tools in my skill belt now.

Climbing over the top of the building and onto the roof was easy enough. The gravel blocks under my feet made landing a little more challenging. I was able to keep my footing lightly enough that I don't think anyone heard me.

Looking around, I immediately found my way in.

Ever since becoming a ninja, there has been one thing that I always wanted to do: Climb into a ventilator shaft. And there just happened to be one poking out of the roof of the building. I removed the iron trapdoor topping it, and slid down into the building.

Building vents are a lot narrower than they seem. The only way I could fit in was to lay flat on my stomach with my arms in front of me, pulling myself forward with my fingertips and toes. Luckily, I didn't make a sound. There was no way anyone would spot me.

I crawled like that until I came over an opening in the vent. I looked down to see where I was.

Jackpot!

I was looking down at Dr. Herobrine's lab.

There were potion bottles with bubbling liquids suspended over brewing stands.

There was a blast furnace with a red-hot fire inside and smoke seeping out the front.

There was redstone dust everywhere, especially on top of all the crafting tables.

Piles of iron ingots were in the corners. And there was a mess of hastily scribbled notes everywhere, on torn pieces of paper, signs, journals, and even on two walls.

I decided to slip out of the vent and see what I could see. However, before I could do that, Dr. Herobrine strolled in with more iron ingots.

Dr. Herobrine was an older looking man, maybe even old enough to be in his 30s. He was wearing a clean white lab coat. Strangely enough, he was also wearing a pair of sunglasses that were almost stuck on his face.

"Catch up!" he ordered to someone behind him. "The sooner we build this Iron Golem, the sooner we can take over the city."

Behind Dr. Herobrine was another ninja! The ninja had their arms full of pumpkins. They were about my size, maybe a little taller, dressed identically to me other than my suit was all black, and theirs was trimmed in red.

I snorted—inside my mind, so they couldn't hear me.

Any real ninja knows you only wear black. Anything other than black, and you might as well be wearing a giant target on yourself. Who would pretend to be a ninja?

"When can I become the lab assistant? I got you all these supplies, so you owe me a promotion!" The ninja's voice was husky, but very definitely feminine.

Dr. Herobrine looked back. "You are not ready to become the lab assistant, Lala. I will let you know when you are ready. Until then, you will still be the lab assistant's lab assistant. L. A. L. A. Lala." He smiled and teasingly booped her nose with his index finger.

"But you don't even have a lab assistant. How can I be the lab assistant's lab assistant, when there is no lab assistant?"

"When I do have one someday, you'll be their assistant," Dr. Herobrine said. "Help me finish unloading the rest of the chests, and maybe–just *maybe*–I'll think about it."

They left through the same door they entered.

They would be back. I probably only had a few minutes to examine the messy lab. Maybe grab a few pieces of paper to bring back to Sensei Setsuo. I quickly opened the vent trapdoor below me and slid out. The next moment I touched down on the floor, staring at Katie and Noodle.

Katie? Noodle?

"Hiya," she said. "How can I help?"

I shushed her, then whispered, "What are you doing in here? I told you to stay outside."

Katie clutched Noodle protectively. "We were," she protested, "but when we saw Dr. Herobrine walk inside, I thought you might need help."

"Well, I don't."

I went to take Katie and Noodle from where they came from, but then I realized I didn't know what direction they came from. "How did you get here? We're on the third floor."

Katie shrugged and innocently looked in any direction except mine.

That was when I realized that she was holding something behind her back.

I held out my hand. "Give it to me."

"What?" she asked.

"Whatever it is you've got there. Hand it over."

She rolled her eyes. "*Fine!*" she said and put it in my hand. "It's the last one I have."

"An ender pearl?" I said, close to yelling. "You teleported up here with an ender pearl! How do you even find one of these?"

Katie sniffed derisively. "You know when you brought me to the Ender Ninjas temple to meet Sensei Setsuo...well...I may have pocketed some cool looking stuff."

After I told Sensei Setsuo that Katie knew my identity and helped me on my first mission, the Sensei wanted to meet her. I had no idea Katie was stealing ender pearls when she was at the dojo. Not to mention as a Wooden Sword rank ninja, even *I* don't get to use the ender pearls yet.

I shoved the ender pearl back at her. "You

take this, you take your chicken, climb out whatever window you crawled through, and you wait for me outside."

Katie pouted. "You are no fun, Nate Noo–Whoops!"

"To control others, you must first control yourself."

- **Miyamoto Musashi**

CHAPTER 7: FAST AND LOOSE

Noodle leapt from Katie's grasp and launched himself out of the room like he was being shot from a crossbow. "Ba-GAWK!"

Katie herself practically squawked when it happened. "Noodle, no!"

She rushed out of the lab, chasing after Noodle. I had no choice but to follow. At this point, I had all of the proof I needed for Sensei Satsuo; I heard Dr. Herobrine say the words "Iron Golem" and saw all the iron ingots and pumpkins he was collecting.

All I had to do was get Katie, Noodle, and myself out of the building without being seen.

CRASH!!!

There went that idea. Something that sounded fragile and valuable fell to the floor in the next room, where Katie and Noodle had run into. As long as nobody saw us, I could still salvage this mission.

"You! A Ninja?! HOW DARE YOU?"

Dr. Herobrine appeared in the other doorway of the lab, his eyes wide and his face red with fury. He was so angry that he shook. He spun on his heels and ran out the door.

A second later, he reappeared and pointed at me again. "Don't go anywhere, you. I'll be back." *Like that was going to happen.* Then he stormed out again.

I quickly started to turn to go into the room with Katie and Noodle, but then I heard Dr. Herobrine's voice from outside.

"Lala! Release the zombies!"

Zombies?

ZOMBIES?!?

I didn't have time to think about that. I sprinted after Katie and Noodle.

The next room was a large kitchen decorated like a restaurant specializing in breakfast. There was a red and white checkered tablecloth on the kitchen table. Utensils hung from the wood block walls.

Noodle flew around the room, sending utensils clattering to the floor. That little chicken had already knocked something like a glass block onto the floor.

That's probably where the noise had come from.

Noodle flapped out of the room through another door. Katie chased after him, and I followed Katie into the hallway outside. There was more wood paneling on the halls.

Noodle continued to knock things down as he careened off the walls in a mad fit. Katie grabbed at Noodle, again and again, only to come back with a fistful of feathers.

Okay, it's ninja time.

Using my mad ninja skills, I zipped past Katie and scooped Noodle up in one arm without slowing my pace toward a large iron door at the end of the hallway.

I slammed straight through the door, opening it on its hinges.

"Stairs! Yes!" I crowed, excited to finally find a way out. Calling over my shoulder, I yelled, "This way!" to Katie.

Inside the stone stairwell, I leapt from landing to landing with Noodle tucked under my arm. Katie followed quickly behind, running down the stairs between floors.

I waited for her to catch up. I didn't want to get too far ahead of her if something happened.

Then something happened.

The door to the first floor opened into a large, dark room, like a warehouse. The only illumination came from torches mounted in the room's corners, spitting harsh-looking shadows on everything.

I saw rows of largish cages all over the floor from what little light I had. With my ninja garb on and my ninja skills, it would be pretty easy to navigate the cages until I found a way out.

Katie would be another matter. She had to stick close by to get out of this maze.

"Noodle, get back over here right this instant!" Katie said sternly.

Noodle wriggled his way out from underneath my arm and eagerly flapped his way to Katie, where he perched contentedly on Katie's shoulder.

"Make sure you don't lose that chicken!" I told Katie.

"It's not my fault, he just likes to run away sometimes!" Katie said.

"Noodle is going to cost us this mission, or *worse*. You have to be more careful with him."

"Maybe if you hadn't yelled at us, Noodle wouldn't have gotten upset."

"Maybe if you had stayed where I told you to—"

"Wait! Do you hear that?" Katie shushed me with her finger and we both listened.

A raspy voice called out to us from the darkness. "Uhhhhh."

The moan of a zombie!

"The first priority to the ninja is to win without fighting."

- **Hatsumi**

CHAPTER 8: SPAWN OF THE DEAD

There was no time to lose. I had to find a way out of there for Katie and Noodle. I would worry about myself later. I climbed to the top of one of the cages to see if I could see into the darkness any better.

I heard the voice again. "Uhhhhhh!"

I realized my mistake immediately. By crawling on top of one of the cages, the zombies could see me better than I could see them. They knew exactly where I was and where Katie and Noodle would be.

However, I did have one thing going for me: Being on top of the cages allowed me to see two doors on the far side of the room.

I heard the scattering of feet around the room as they started coming towards us.

How are there so many of them? It's like we walked right into...wait a second...

DIARY OF NATE THE MINECRAFT NINJA 2

I looked at the cage I was standing on. It wasn't just an ordinary cage. It was a monster spawner.

I had learned about these contraptions in ninja training. Mystical cages that can spawn mobs, including those that can spawn zombies!

We were probably surrounded by a horde of them.

I had to turn the zombie hoard away from Katie as quickly as possible. Fortunately for me, most of the cages were of the same size so that I could run on the tops of the cages easily. Hopefully, whatever was out there would follow me instead of going after Katie.

"Katie, throw me the chicken!"

Katie hurled Noodle at me from the ground. Then I helped Katie up too.

I explained that I wanted her and Noodle to run on the cages to one of the exit doors. In contrast, I will run towards the other and try to get the zombies to follow me.

"Got all that?"

Katie is practically fearless, and Noodle even more so. Katie snapped a salute at me. "Yessir!"

I didn't have time to make sure she understood, so I nodded and started running towards one of the doors while she took off in the other direction.

"Come on zombies! Get over here!" I clanked my wooden sword on the cages below me.

My eyes must have gotten used to the lack of light because I slowly began to make out other shapes in the darkness. Shapes that looked like arms and hands reaching up to grab me. There was also the scattering sound of dozens of tiny feet running on the floors around me.

I didn't stay still long enough for any of them to catch me, but the hands seemed to reach out forever. The sound of more and more voices echoed around me. "Uhhhhh!"

I needed to jump over the zombies to the next row of cages before making it to the door. I found a nice, tall cage to jump from and leapt—or intended to, anyway.

Instead, a hand reached out from behind to grab my leg. I fell forward over the front of the tall cage and hung over the edge. I stared directly into the eyes of a zombie as it unhinged its jaw and approached my face.

I got yanked back up to the safety of the top of the cage. I flipped over, prepared to kick whatever zombie had tripped me square in his zombie face.

Instead, I came face-to-face with Lala, the red ninja. She jumped up and back by at least five feet without seeming to move at all. Her eyes never left mine.

However amateurish her red garb was. She was definitely a ninja. She had the training. She stood there in a defensive walking stance, waiting for me to make the first move. A ninja fights only when they have to. That is the ninja way.

I turned to jump over to the next row of cages like my plan had been all along, but in the split second it took me to glance over and prepare myself for the jump, she tackled me.

I landed flat on my back with Lala on top of me. She began throwing a flurry of rapid blows at my head that I was only *just* barely able to block to prevent my face from being rearranged.

From my prone position, I swung my legs up and around Lala's shoulders and flung her backwards over several cages before she landed on her butt many feet away.

I flipped myself off my back into a spider stance. I waved my hand forward, inviting her to catch me off guard again.

Come at me, bro.

Suddenly all the lights in the room came to life in a quick series of sizzling pops. I noticed the glowstone lights were powered by redstone, just before they blinded me for a moment.

Lala came at me, bro, and slapped me hard with a roundhouse kick to the face.

"Sorry!" Katie yelled at me from across the room. She stood by an open door that went outside. "Found the lights," she added helpfully while pointing to a lever.

Unlike Lala and me, Katie wasn't wearing a mask. I couldn't let Lala see her face. I reached into my pocket and slammed a sand block right into Lala's face. No one can see with sand in their eyes, even ninjas.

"Go!" I shouted.

"Noodle!" Katie yelped.

I looked to see that a tiny baby zombie was trying to jockey with Noodle. I quickly threw an arrow to knock the baby zombie off. But just then, another baby zombie jumped right back onto Noodle.

Apparently, all the baby zombies wanted to jockey with Noodle.

"Get. Off. My. Chicken." Katie yelled as she kicked and punched the baby zombies away.

I tried to throw some more arrows, but Lala sent a punch to my kidney, doubling me over. I was quick enough to block a chop to my neck and bounced backward to give myself a little breathing space.

Lala had rubbed the sand out and she could see again. I quickly turned to see if Katie and Noodle were safe, and thankfully it was nice to see Katie and Noodle had gotten out safely.

Now I just had to be able to do it myself. Lala was blocking my direct path. I'd have to go over her, around her, or through her to get to the exit door.

I chose the third.

I decided that what I needed to do was to go a little old school on Lala. I lowered my shoulder and barreled at her to knock her off the cages and into the zombies below.

Lala dodged me by jumping straight up and letting me rumble beneath her before landing gently with a kick. With my center of gravity off point, I tumbled and came to a rest lying precariously over the edge of one cage.

How many times had I found myself on the ground since the fight started? Three?

I had to admit it, she could do things that I hadn't learned yet. She was better than me. She didn't have a sword, so I didn't even know what rank she was.

I had to get out of there and now.

A hand in a ragged shirt grabbed my garb at the

shoulder and started pulling me off the cage.

Nope, I was not going down today. I still had to ask out Min. I was not going to allow myself to die until I accomplished at least that. So, I reached out for the hand grabbing me and felt something cold and fleshy.

I turned around and I was looking into the face of a vicious looking zombie. The zombie growled at me and started going in for a bite, like a toddler with a slice of cake.

I was able to yank myself away just in time to keep my face from being removed, but the zombie ripped off a piece of my garb and left a nasty scrape on my skin. It would leave a nasty scab in the morning… if I could fight my way out to see the next morning.

Jumping back to my feet, Lala was behind me, just staring at me. She was confused like she suddenly didn't know what to do next.

I took that as my cue to go. I took a running leap over the heads of several of the zombies that surrounded me and bounded out the door.

On the other side, Katie and Noodle waited.

"Hold on to me!" Katie yelled.

I didn't know what she was thinking, but I listened to her. I grabbed onto her tight.

"This is my last one!" Katie said as she tossed the ender pearl as far away as she could.

For the first time in my life, I realized how good of a thrower Katie is. Maybe slamming lockers built up her strength just for this moment.

The ender pearl landed far away, and teleported all three of us into safer neighborhoods. Despite that, we kept running for a while.

Katie was out of breath, and it didn't appear as though anyone was following us, so we slowed to a stop a couple of blocks away from our homes, and Katie pulled out her water bottle to take a swig.

Wiping her mouth dry with the back of her sleeve, she asked me, "So is that what being a ninja is really like?"

I laughed in spite of myself. "Yeah. We can go back tomorrow night and do it again if you want to."

Katie's eyes lit up, and she got a wild smile on her face. "Yes!"

"I...wasn't being serious."

"All's well that ends well."
-    **Shakespeare**

CHAPTER 9: EPILOGUE

"So, what did Sensei say?"

Katie and I were at our lockers getting ready for our first classes of the day. Noodle was comfy on the shelf in Katie's locker, indifferent to escaping for the moment. At least, Noodle was behaving today.

I told Katie that I had surprised Sensei Satsuo when I told him I had battled a ninja in a roomful of zombies. He was more surprised with the ninja part than the zombie part.

He had said that there were no other ninjas in Central City as far as he knew and that he'd look into it. Apparently, in the Ender Ninja order, every city usually only has one master ninja and one apprentice ninja.

He also said that he'd continue to work on making sure we track down any other deliveries to Dr. Herobrine.

"Wow," Katie said. "That's... anti-climactic."

I shrugged. It was what it was. At the end of the day, even ninjas had to fill out paperwork.

"So, what are you going to do about her?" Katie asked me.

Min and her gaggle of friends strolled past Katie and me. I had a newfound confidence. I had just fought off a plague of zombies and an unknown ninja.

I could ask a girl out to the dance. Couldn't I?

"Hey Min!" I said, stopping her in her tracks.

"Hey Nate!" Min smiled. "Before you ask, I think the weather's great out today. Lovely clouds too."

"Oh..." I blushed. "I...actually...had a different question to ask you."

"Go ahead, shoot," Min leaned forward, maybe I was speaking quietly because I was nervous.

"So, the Fall Ball is coming up, and I was wondering if you would...you know...like someone to go with. Someone like me."

"Oh, I'm sorry, Nate," Min said a few moments later after I'd asked her. "I already said yes to somebody else. But if you had asked me yesterday, I would have said yes to you instead. Can you believe everyone's been so intimidated by me, that no one had asked me till yesterday?"

"Oh—"

Before I could say anything else, Min's friends dragged her away so they could continue whatever conversation they were having.

I reported back to Katie. Her response was to say, "I take it all back... now *that* was anti-climactic. What are you going to do now?"

"I don't know. Want to go to the Fall Ball with me?"

"Will you bring me flowers and some seeds for Noodle?"

"Sure, I guess."

"I'd love to."

DIARY OF NATE THE MINECRAFT NINJA 3

Middle School ninja Nate Noonan heads to the first field trip of the school year. This year the kids are headed to Snow Spook Mountain. With rumors of an evil snowman roaming the dark mountainside, Nate hopes taking down the monster might be his best chance at earning the Stone Sword rank. Will Nate succeed or is the mystery behind the mountain too much for one young ninja to handle?

Check it out:

Diary of Nate the Minecraft Ninja 3

https://www.amazon.com/dp/B09ZPMLD76

A NOTE FROM WRITE BLOCKED:

I hope you all enjoyed the second book of my brand-new series *Diary of Nate the Minecraft Ninja!* I hope you're enjoying the series so far. Make sure to leave a review, so I know what you think and what you want to see next. You can also leave character ideas and I'll try to add them to future books! You can also become a part of the Order of the Reviewer Ninjas!

Right now, I'm working on *Diary of Nate the Minecraft Ninja 3*. I think you guys will enjoy this next adventure a lot!

There are more exciting things in the works, so make sure you join the newsletter to stay up to date with everything.

Well, to finish off this note, I'll just say I hope you enjoyed reading this book as much as I enjoyed writing it. I can't wait to read your reviews and see what you think!

(NEW) Join the group on Goodreads: https://www.goodreads.com/group/1173039

Follow Me on Twitter: https://twitter.com/writeblocked

Follow me on Instagram: http://instagram.com/writeblocked

Join the Discord Fan Group: https://discord.gg/FAFWz7g

Subscribe to my Newsletter: https://tinyletter.com/WriteBlocked

My Email if you wish to contact me: WriteBlockedOfficial@gmail.com

MY QUESTIONS
FOR YOU!

Answer one, answer two, or answer all! It's up to you!

Who would you take to the Fall Ball, Katie or Min?

Do you want to see more of the red ninja, codenamed: Lala?

Have you ever seen a ghost?

THE ORDER OF THE REVIEWER NINJAS!

Wooden Sword Rank Ninjas

- Cløtret

Guide:

Wooden Sword Rank Ninjas (1 Review)

Stone Sword Rank Ninjas (2 Reviews)

Iron Sword Rank Ninjas (3 Reviews)

Diamond Sword Rank Ninjas (4 Reviews)

Netherite Sword Rank Ninjas (5 Reviews)

Me When You Leave A Review

Me When You Don't Review

Love Minecraft? Love Superheroes? Check out The Mob Hunter!

A deadly creeper attack left Steve for dead, but saved by Apollo Technologies, he was put back together using different parts of different mobs. He has the strength of a zombie. The aim of a skeleton. The teleportation of an enderman. And the ability to blow himself up of a creeper.

He is Minecraft's First Superhero: The Mob Hunter!

https://www.amazon.com/dp/B08BRTR7PW

How would you survive if you got Stuck Inside Minecraft?

Michael is an average struggling Twitch streamer, but things get un-average pretty quickly when he is teleported inside the world of Minecraft. Things only get crazier when he finds out that he is the prophesied savior of Minecraft.

Join Michael as he saves the world!

https://www.amazon.com/dp/B08CTB7KQZ

Welcome to Monster Middle School!
A Complete Series!

https://www.amazon.com/gp/product/B08SW53D32

Love Minecraft and funny stories? Check out my
other diary title: Diary of a Half Zombie

https://www.amazon.com/dp/B015S4X5R2

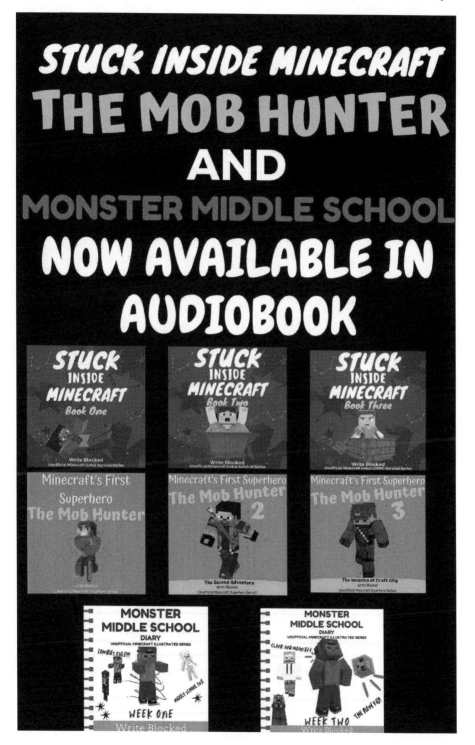

Stuck Inside Minecraft, The Mob Hunter, Timmy The Traveler and Monster Middle School are now on audiobook!

Listen to your favorite characters brought to life by professional voice actors!

How do Michael, Jack, Emma, and The Mob Hunter sound like on their adventures?

And the question everyone's been asking: What does Paul's rap really sound like?

You can purchase the audiobook version of these books on Amazon, iTunes, or on Aubdible. You can even listen to them for free by opening an Aubdible Free Trial Membership!

The Mob Hunter 1: Audible
The Mob Hunter 2: Audible
The Mob Hunter 3: Audible
The Mob Hunter 4: Audible

Stuck Inside Minecraft Book 1: Audible
Stuck Inside Minecraft Book 2: Audible
Stuck Inside Minecraft Book 3: Audible
Stuck Inisde Minecraft Book 4: Audible
Stuck Inside Minecraft Book 5: Audible

Monster Middle School Week 1: Audible
Monster Middle School Week 2: Audible

Timmy The Traveler - Lies in London: Audible
Timmy The Traveler - Nefarious in New York: Audible

ACKNOWLEDGEMENT

This book would not be possible without your continued support. A big thank you to the fans.

ABOUT THE AUTHOR

Write Blocked

Check out all the other amazing minecraft books by Write Blocked on Amazon!

Diary of Nate the Minecraft Ninja

The Mob Hunter Series

Diary of a Minecraft Half Zombie Series

Stuck Inside Minecraft Series

Stuck Inside Minecraft: Pocket Edition Series

Timmy The Traveler Series

Monster Middle School Diary Series

BOOKS BY THIS AUTHOR

The Mob Hunter Series

A deadly creeper attack left Steve for dead, but saved by Apollo Technologies, he was put back together using different parts of different mobs.

He has the strength of a zombie.

The aim of a skeleton.

The teleportation of an enderman.

And the ability to blow himself up of a creeper. Hey, you never know.

Follow the Mob Hunter is his various adventures

Stuck Inside Minecraft Series

Michael is an average struggling Twitch streamer, but things get un-average pretty quickly when he is teleported inside the world of Minecraft. Things only get crazier when he finds out that he is the prophesied savior of Minecraft.

Follow Michael, Jack, and Emma in their adventures inside the world of Minecraft!

Timmy The Traveler Series

Join famed adventurer Timmy The Traveler and his pet parrot Penny in their first epic adventure. Part adventure, and part mystery, this is the newest series from Write Blocked.

In this adventure Timmy finds himself in London where he must team up with Sherblock Holmes and his pet pig Watson to solve a mystery!

Diary Of A Minecraft Half Zombie Series

You've heard of Zombies, Skeletons, Creepers, Endermen, but you've never heard of the Half Zombie. This, totally real, diary was written by Chewy Walker. Chewy Walker has always been different. He's been a nerd, an outcast and of course a half zombie. But today, all of that is going to change. Chewy is going on a journey to become a full blown zombie.

He'll meet wacky friends, and even wackier enemies. With mind blowing twists, and pants pooping hilarious moments, this is one Minecraft book you do NOT want to miss.

Check out one of the most exciting Minecraft books on the market and get ready to go on one epic journey.

This book features over a dozen fully colored original images!

Monster Middle School Diary Series

Follow the adventures of a group of zany kids in Monster Middle School as they learn about friendship and try their best to survive middle school! These books feature over 40 illustrations per book and have laugh out loud moments for the whole family. Start reading today!

Stuck Inside Minecraft: Pocket Edition

Pari Patel, Denzel Brown, and Aiden Smith are regular kids playing Minecraft: Pocket Edition on the school bus in one moment, and in the next, they are stuck inside Minecraft with no way out.

Little do they know these young kids have been chosen as heroes in a conflict inside the world of Minecraft and only while working together can they hope to save themselves and the world.

Spinning off the pages of Stuck Inside Minecraft comes a brand-new spin-off series with a new story and a new cast. You can read this new series without having read the original series!

You don't want to miss this adventure!

Made in the USA
Columbia, SC
14 November 2023

26264606R00057